W9-AQX-178

Copyright © 2021 by Gracey Zhang
All rights reserved. Published by Orchard Books, an imprint of Scholastic Inc., *Publishers since 1920*. ORCHARD BOOKS and design are registered trademarks of Watts Publishing Group, Ltd., used under license. SCHOLASTIC and associated logos are trademarks and/or registered trademarks of Scholastic Inc. • The publisher does not have any control over and does not assume any responsibility for author or third-party websites or their content. • No part of this publication may be reproduced, stored in a retrieval system, or transmitted in any form or by any means, electronic, mechanical, photocopying, recording, or otherwise, without written permission of the publisher. For information regarding permission, write to Scholastic Inc., Attention: Permissions Department, 557 Broadway, New York, NY 10012. • This book is a work of fiction. Names, characters, places, and incidents are either the product of the author's imagination or are used fictitiously, and any resemblance to actual persons, living or dead, business establishments, events, or locales is entirely coincidental.

Library of Congress Cataloging-in-Publication Data available
ISBN 978-1-338-64823-2
10 9 8 7 6 5 4 3 2 1   21 22 23 24 25
Printed in China   62
First edition, April 2021

LALA'S WORDS

by Gracey Zhang

Orchard Books
An Imprint of Scholastic Inc.
New York

Hot, hot, hot.
The sidewalks steamed and the sun hung heavy in the sky.
Everyone was still.

Lala was not.

Lala jumped

and ran,

tripped

and fell.

Lala was sweaty and her clothes always torn.

"Lala, stay still!" her mother said.

"What child is as rough as you?"

Lala didn't know. But she did know she liked to go outside.
Past Mr. Piatek with his radio. Around the corner, down the block . . .

. . . over the fence, in a patch
of dirt and concrete, grew
short green weeds and leaves.

A place of Lala's own.

"Hello, hello, friends,"
Lala whispered.

Every morning Lala ran to her garden.

Through the heat she carried a pot of water, but it was
her kind words that made the plants sway and nod.

"You are stripy and lovely," said Lala.

"Stop playing with weeds and leaves!
You're covered in dirt!" cried her mother.

"Grow strong and tall, my friends," said Lala.

"Be still and quiet,"
said her mother.

"You are so very special,"
sighed Lala.

On the hottest day of summer, Lala's mother had enough.

"No more, Lala! No more jibber-jabber in dirt and grass!
Today you are staying at home."

Lala cried and cried.
Who would visit her little friends?

So Lala stayed inside, out from the melting heat.
From the window she counted buses wheezing past,
listened to Mr. Piatek hum with his radio, and waved
politely when Rosie passed by with their groceries.

Throughout the day she whispered softly,
"Hello, hello, friends."

At night the moon rose like a bright eye.
Out her window Lala whispered to her plants,
"Goodnight, my friends, I love you very much."

The next morning the sun didn't burn so strong.
It was cool, cool, cool and breezy under a great big shade.

Héctor was the first to see. When he looked out his window,
he whistled long and hard. "Well look at that!"

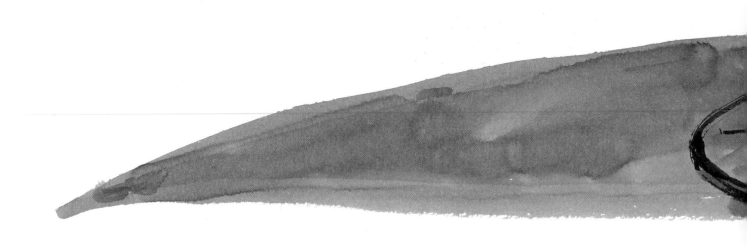

Lala's friends had grown strong and tall. So strong and tall, they covered Lala and her neighbors like a fountain under the sun.

They had been listening every day that summer.
So deeply they listened to Lala's words, they had
come to find her through the warm night air.

"Magnificent, my magnificent friends!" cried Lala.

Lala ran down the stairs.
Her mother was staring out the door.

"Oh, Lala . . ."

"... you are so very special."

Her mother held her close and tight, and Lala felt warm inside.

"I love you, my amazing girl.
Go out and play."

And Lala did.

To the Lala in all of us.
— GZ

Gracey Zhang's illustrations were created using ink and gouache.
The text type was set in Caslon. The display type was hand lettered by Gracey Zhang.
The book was printed on 160 gsm Golden Sun woodfree and bound at Leo Paper.
Production was overseen by Catherine Weening. Manufacturing was supervised by Shannon Rice.
The book was art directed by Patti Ann Harris, designed by Doan Buu, and edited by Kait Feldmann.